**Don't bend my ear!**

# On To Widecombe Fair

# On To Widecombe Fair

by Patricia Lee Gauch · illustrated by Trina Schart Hyman

G. P. Putnam's Sons · New York

FOR ALL THE HAPPY CREATURES AT OLD WALLS
AND FOR ARLETTA, OF COURSE.

P.L.G.

Library of Congress Cataloging in Publication Data
Gauch, Patricia Lee. On to Widecombe Fair.
SUMMARY: Seven men who don't like to walk borrow
an old mare to ride to the Widecombe fair.
[1. Folklore—England]   I. Hyman, Trina Schart.   II. Title.
PZ8.1.G168701   813'.5'4 [398.2] [E]   76-48151
ISBN 0-399-20563-2

FOR MOLLIE AND AILSA AND JAY
· WITH THANKS AND LOVE ·

TSH

I have been to Widecombe, and I have a story to tell, and as I have been to Widecombe, I can assure you, it is all perfectly, absolutely, unquestionably true.

Long ago, that means before your grandmother's grandmother made her eat *her* porridge, Widecombe was tucked into the moors (just as it is now), all crusty stone shops (just as they are now), a village green that the cows knew perfectly well they owned (just as they do now), and a prim church three times the size of the rest of the village. (It's the same way now.)

Most days it was a quiet little village except on fair day, that once-a-year-day when stalls and people and sheep and goodies sprouted in the village like wild flowers in May. Just thinking of Widecombe Fair made the country folk's mouths water and their spirits fly.

No one wanted to miss it.

Certainly not Bill Brewer, Jan Stewer, Peter Gurney, Peter Davey, Dan'l Widden, Harry Hawke or old Uncle Tom Cobley. But they—Bill Brewer, Jan Stewer, Peter Gurney, Peter Davey, Dan'l Widden, Harry Hawke and old Uncle Tom Cobley—lived very nearly all the way to Spreyton—a terrible long walk indeed.

And they were talking men—not walking men!

So, on the day of the fair, being sensible fellows,
they gathered in town and willy-nilly piled into Tom's wagon.
But his wagon broke down.
They climbed into Dan's cart.
But his donkey wouldn't pull.

They thought there might be room in a passing coach.
But, dear me, there wasn't.
It was then that they spied Tom Pearse's grey mare, his very old
grumpy grey mare, napping under a tree.

"Aw," said Peter Davey to Tom Pearse himself, "what a purty old creature, she."

"Yesss," crooned Bill Brewer and Jan Stewer, "a beauty, for certain."

"And sturdy, as well," said Peter Gurney, Dan'l Widden, Harry Hawke, old Uncle Tom Cobley and all.

"Aye," said Tom Pearse and just that, for he was a walking man, not a talking man.

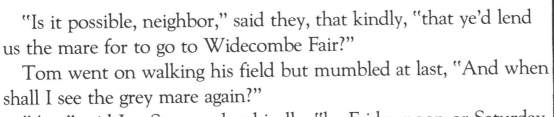

"Is it possible, neighbor," said they, that kindly, "that ye'd lend us the mare for to go to Widecombe Fair?"

Tom went on walking his field but mumbled at last, "And when shall I see the grey mare again?"

"Aw," said Jan Stewer, that kindly, "by Friday noon or Saturday soon."

And Tom went on walking but nodded aye.

So off they set with the mare willy-nilly, but being sensible fellows, on the way to the fair, they took turns.

Bill Brewer, he trotted to Whiddon Down.

Jan Stewer took his turn to Chagford.

Peter Gurney and Peter Davey shared the hills to Beetor Cross (one up and one down).

Dan'l Widden and Harry Hawke rode to Heatree.

And old Uncle Tom Cobley jogged into the fair.

And, oh, what they saw there! Across from the sheep and stalls, tents spread over the field like giant umbrellas, and under them and between them were people—rosy-cheeked people—singing and shouting and dancing and laughing and eating and drinking....

So baskey-eyed and market merry, they—Jan Stewer, Bill Brewer, Peter Gurney, Peter Davey, Dan'l Widden, Harry Hawke and old Uncle Tom Cobley—started doing the same, and more.

They danced with young maid Nell and old maid Betsy, two at a time. And they talked.

They played bowls with Farmer Fursdon, winning some and losing some. And they talked.

 They raced John Oke's pony Ann and his sheep Sue. And they talked.

They stuffed themselves with gingerbread jumble, fairing cake, cinnamon sweets, and they drank the bubbly Widecombe brew. And then they talked and talked and talked!

Until Friday was gone and Saturday very nearly was, too.

But, oh, they had to get back by Saturday close, and, so, they ran to the mare willy-nilly, but stuffed with the goodies and brew, they were not the same sensible fellows.

"I s'll go first," said Jan Stewer, hopping on the old mare's back.
"Good," said Bill Brewer. "I, too."
"And I," said Peter Gurney and Peter Davey.
"And I! And I! And I!" said the rest.

Until finally Tom Pearse's old mare—his very old grumpy grey mare—was seen plodding away from the fair with them all on her back at once.

"A purty old creature, she!" shouted Jan Stewer, who was the first of the first.

"A bea-uty!" said Bill Brewer, who was second of the first.

"And sturdy, as well," said Peter Gurney. And Peter Davey, Dan'l Widden, Harry Hawke and old Uncle Tom Cobley agreed.

Over and over and over they agreed.

Now, Tom Pearse, when Saturday started slipping away, started walking to Widecombe to look for his old grey mare. So, as the others were trotting to Heatree Cross, Tom, he was walking to Whiddon.

As they wandered down Long Lane, Tom had just passed Chagford. And as they started up the hill at Beetor, Tom, he started down.

But it was Tom who spied them first, and no longer plodding uphill. There, stopped in the middle of the road were Bill Brewer, Jan Stewer, Peter Gurney, Peter Davey, Dan'l Widden, Harry Hawke, old Uncle Tom Cobley and all, pleading with Tom Pearse's grey mare to get up. (You see, she was down on her knees a-making her will.)

As they pleaded, they listened and tapped and shook their heads, but no coaxing would change her mind. For as they listened and tapped and shook their heads, the old mare stubbornly rolled over and died.

"A purty old creature," sobbed Jan Stewer.

"A beauty, for certain," sighed Bill Brewer.

"And sturdy, as well," groaned Peter Gurney, Peter Davey,
Dan'l Widden, Harry Hawke, old Uncle Tom Cobley and all.

"Aye," said Tom Pearse, and he sat down on a stone, and he cried.

But this wasn't the end of Tom Pearse's grey mare. I have been to Widecombe and I know, for when the wind whistles cold on the moors of a night, Tom Pearse's grey mare appears, grinning ghostly and white.

Talk as they might, there's no getting off for old Uncle Tom Cobley and all.

The story was based on this folk song which, as you can see, carries even one more passenger, the singer of the song.

1. Tom Pearse, Tom Pearse, lend me your grey mare, all along, down a-long out a-long lee. For I

2. And when shall I see a-gain my grey mare? All along, down a-long out a-long lee. By

want for to go - to Widecombe Fair, with Bill Brewer, Jan Stewer, Peter Gurney, Peter Davey Dan'l

Fri - day noon or Saturday soon, with Bill Brewer, Jan Stewer, Peter Gurney, Peter Davey Dan'l

Widden, Harry Hawke, Old Uncle Tom Cobley and all, . . . Old Uncle Tom Cobley and all .

Widden, Harry Hawke, Old Uncle Tom Cobley and all, . . . Old Uncle Tom Cobley and all .

UNCLE TOM COBLEY     GREY MARE     TOM PEARSE     "ALL"

3. Then Friday came and Saturday soon,
    All along, down along, out along lee.
But Tom Pearse's old mare has not trotted home,
With Bill Brewer, Jan Stewer, Peter Gurney,
    Peter Davey, Dan'l Widden, Harry Hawke,
Old Uncle Tom Cobley and all,
    Old Uncle Tom Cobley and all.

4. So Tom Pearse he got up to the top of the hill,
    All along, down along, out along lee.
And he seed his old mare down a'making her will,
With Bill Brewer, Jan Stewer, Peter Gurney,
    Peter Davey, Dan'l Widden, Harry Hawke,
Old Uncle Tom Cobley and all,
    Old Uncle Tom Cobley and all.

5. So Tom Pearse's old mare her took sick and died,
    All along, down along, out along lee.
And Tom he sat down on a stone and he cried,
With Bill Brewer, Jan Stewer, Peter Gurney,
    Peter Davey, Dan'l Widden, Harry Hawke,
Old Uncle Tom Cobley and all,
    Old Uncle Tom Cobley and all.

6. But this isn't the end of this shocking affair,
    All along, down along, out along lee.
Nor though they be dead of the horrid career,
With Bill Brewer, Jan Stewer, Peter Gurney,
    Peter Davey, Dan'l Widden, Harry Hawke,
Old Uncle Tom Cobley and all,
    Old Uncle Tom Cobley and all.

7. When the wind whistles cold on the moor of a night,
    All along, down along, out along lee.
Tom Pearse's old mare doth appear ghastly white,
With Bill Brewer, Jan Stewer, Peter Gurney,
    Peter Davey, Dan'l Widden, Harry Hawke,
Old Uncle Tom Cobley and all,
    Old Uncle Tom Cobley and all.

8. And all the long night be heard skirling and groans,
    All along, down along, out along lee.
From Tom Pearse's old mare and a rattling of bones,
With Bill Brewer, Jan Stewer, Peter Gurney,
    Peter Davey, Dan'l Widden, Harry Hawke,
Old Uncle Tom Cobley and all,
    Old Uncle Tom Cobley and all.